Your child's love of reading starts here, with HarperAlley's **I Can Read** *Comics*!

HARPER *alley*

MW01062810

I Can Read *Comics* introduces children to the world of graphic novel storytelling and encourages visual literacy in emerging readers. Comics inspire reader engagement unlike any other format. They ask readers to infer and answer questions, like:

1. What do I read first? Image or text?
2. Why is this word balloon shaped this way, and that word balloon shaped that way?
3. Why is a character making that facial expression? Are they happy, angry, excited, sad?

From the comics your child reads with you to the first comic they read on their own, there are **I Can Read** *Comics* for every stage of reading:

LEVEL 1
Simple stories for shared reading.

LEVEL 2
Engaging stories for children reading on their own.

LEVEL 3
Complex stories for independent readers.

The magic of graphic novel storytelling lies between the gutters.
Unlock the magic with…

I Can Read *Comics*!

Visit **ICanRead.com** for information on enriching your child's reading experience.

I Can Read *Comics* Cartooning Basics

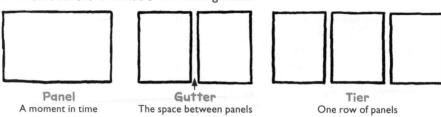

Panel
A moment in time

Gutter
The space between panels

Tier
One row of panels

Word Balloons When someone talks, thinks, whispers, or screams, their words go in here:

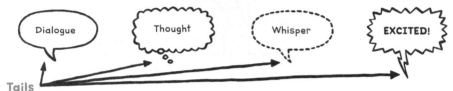

Dialogue

Thought

Whisper

EXCITED!

Tails
Point to whoever is talking / thinking / whispering / screaming / etc.

A quick how-to-read comics guide:

In a **panel**, read the text on the **left** first.

Then, read the text on the **right**.

Remember to...
Read the text along with the image, paying close attention to the character's acting, the action, and/or the scene. Every little detail matters!

No dialogue? No problem!
If there is no dialogue within a panel, take the time to read the image. Visual cues are just as important as text, so don't forget about them!

On a page, **start here**, in the **top left** corner!

After that, read the panel immediately to the **right**.

When you're done up there, come down here and read **this** panel **next**!

ME NEXT! ME NEXT!

You're almost there...

YOU MADE IT! You just read a comic page!

YAY!

HarperAlley is an imprint of HarperCollins Publishers.
I Can Read® and I Can Read Book® are trademarks of HarperCollins Publishers.

Pete the Cat and the Space Chase
Text copyright © 2023 by Kimberly and James Dean
Illustrations copyright © 2023 by James Dean
Pete the Cat is a registered trademark of Pete the Cat, LLC.

Library of Congress Control Number: 2023932464
ISBN 978-0-06-297443-3 (trade bdg.) — ISBN 978-0-06-297439-6 (pbk.)

Book design by Rick Farley and Jon Corby
24 25 26 27 CWM 10 9 8 7   First Edition

I Can Read! Comics
LEVEL 1

Pete the Cat and the Space Chase

by Kimberly & James Dean

HARPER alley
An Imprint of HarperCollinsPublishers

Meet Pete the Cat...

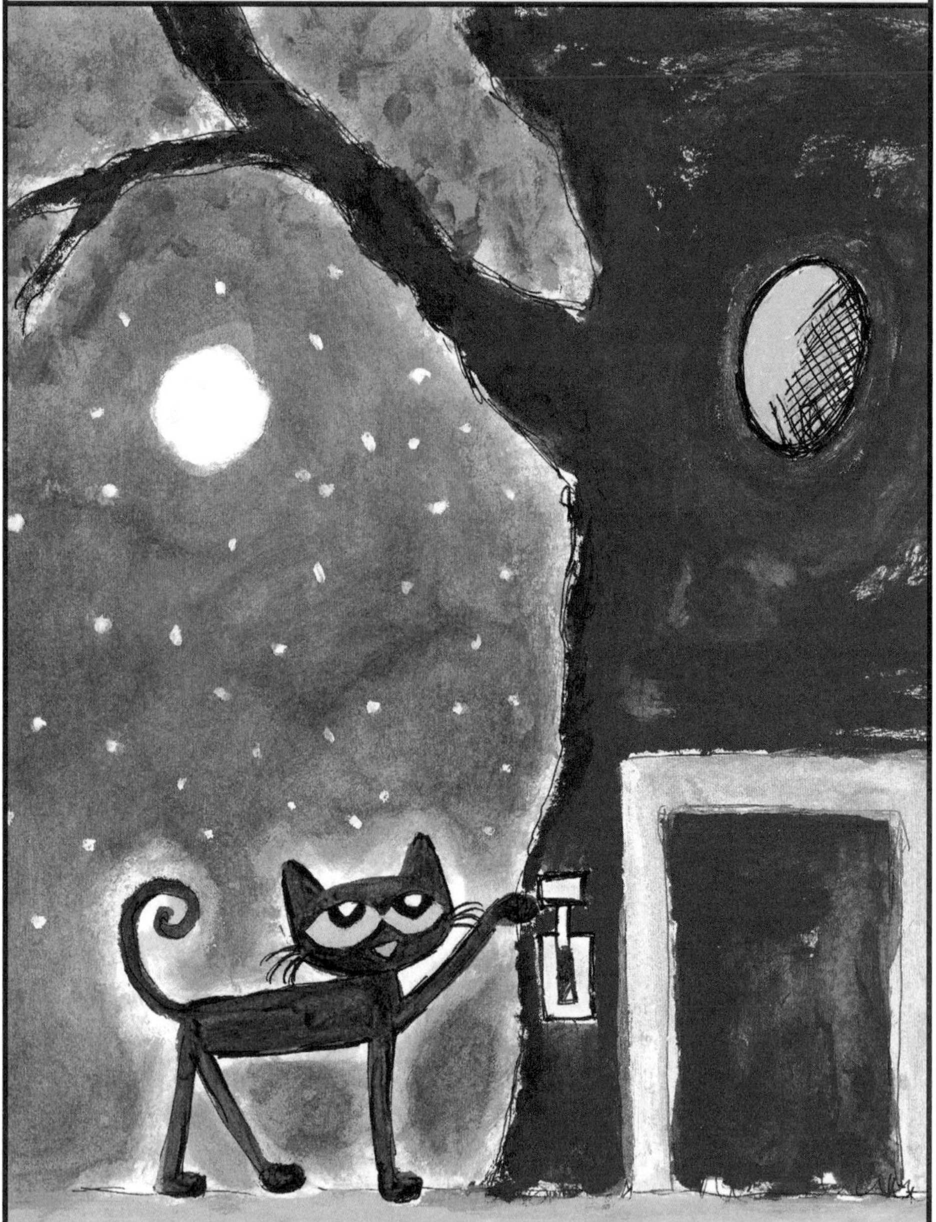

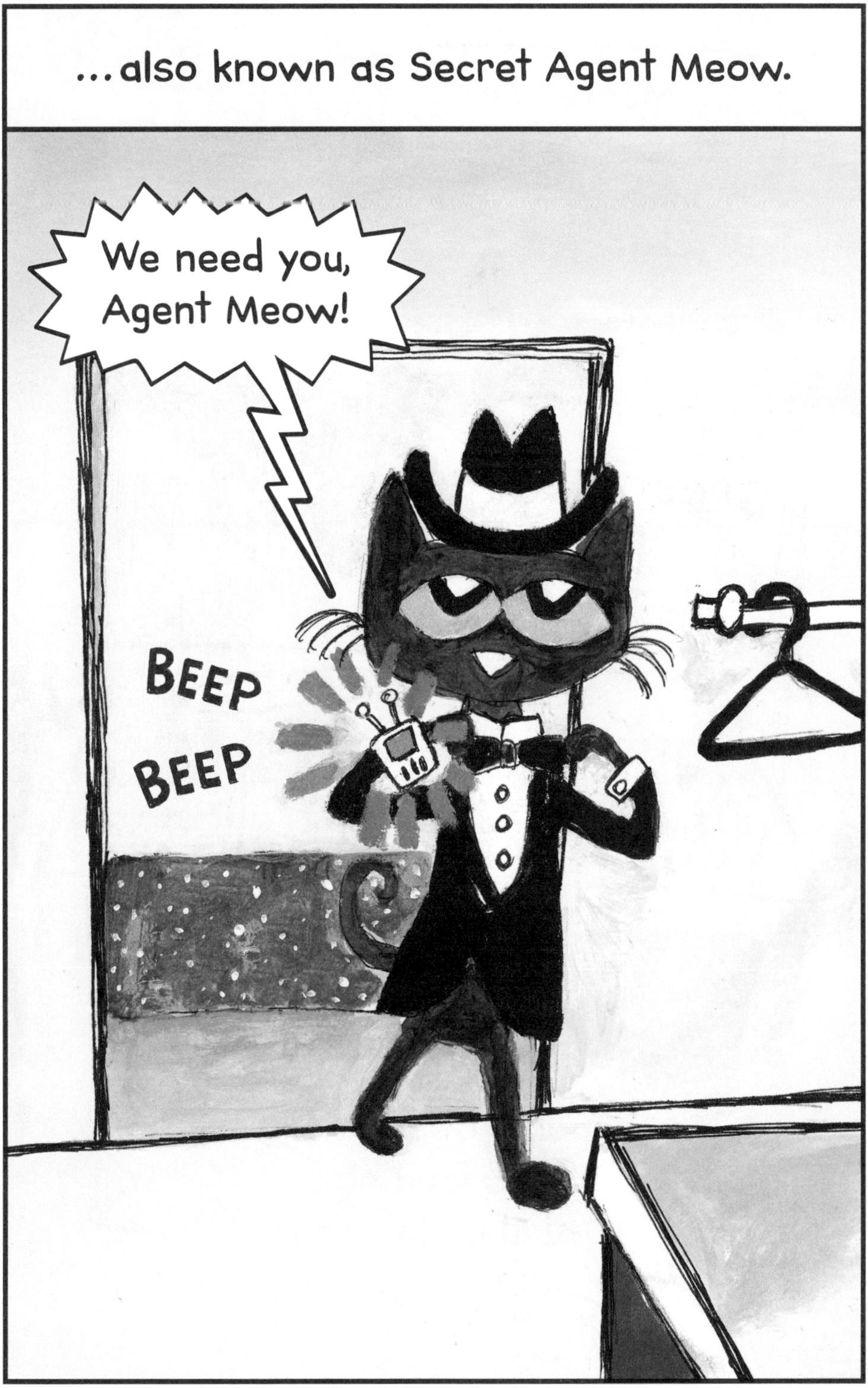
...also known as Secret Agent Meow.
We need you, Agent Meow!
BEEP
BEEP

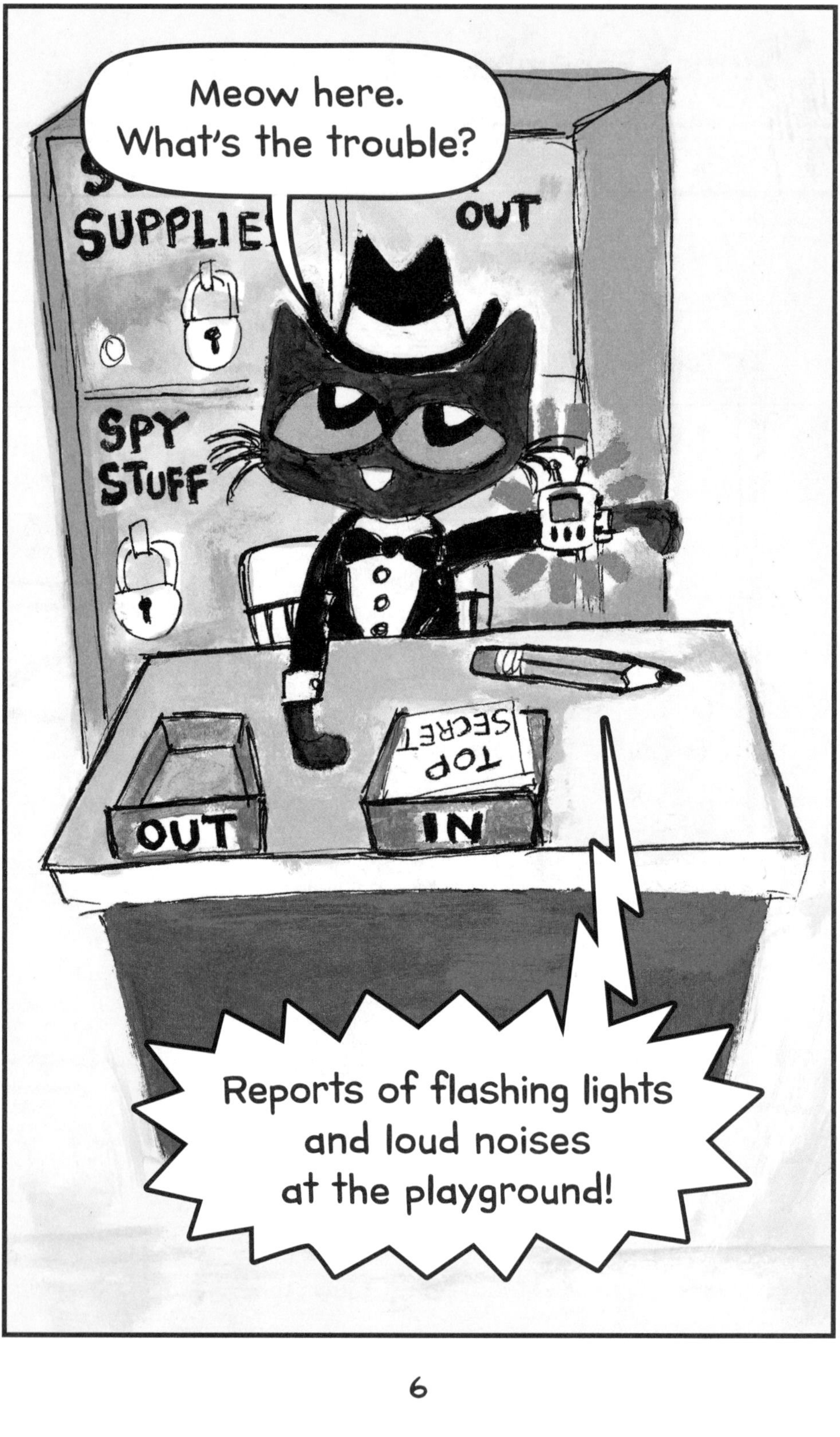
Meow here. What's the trouble?
Reports of flashing lights and loud noises at the playground!
SPY STUFF
OUT
IN

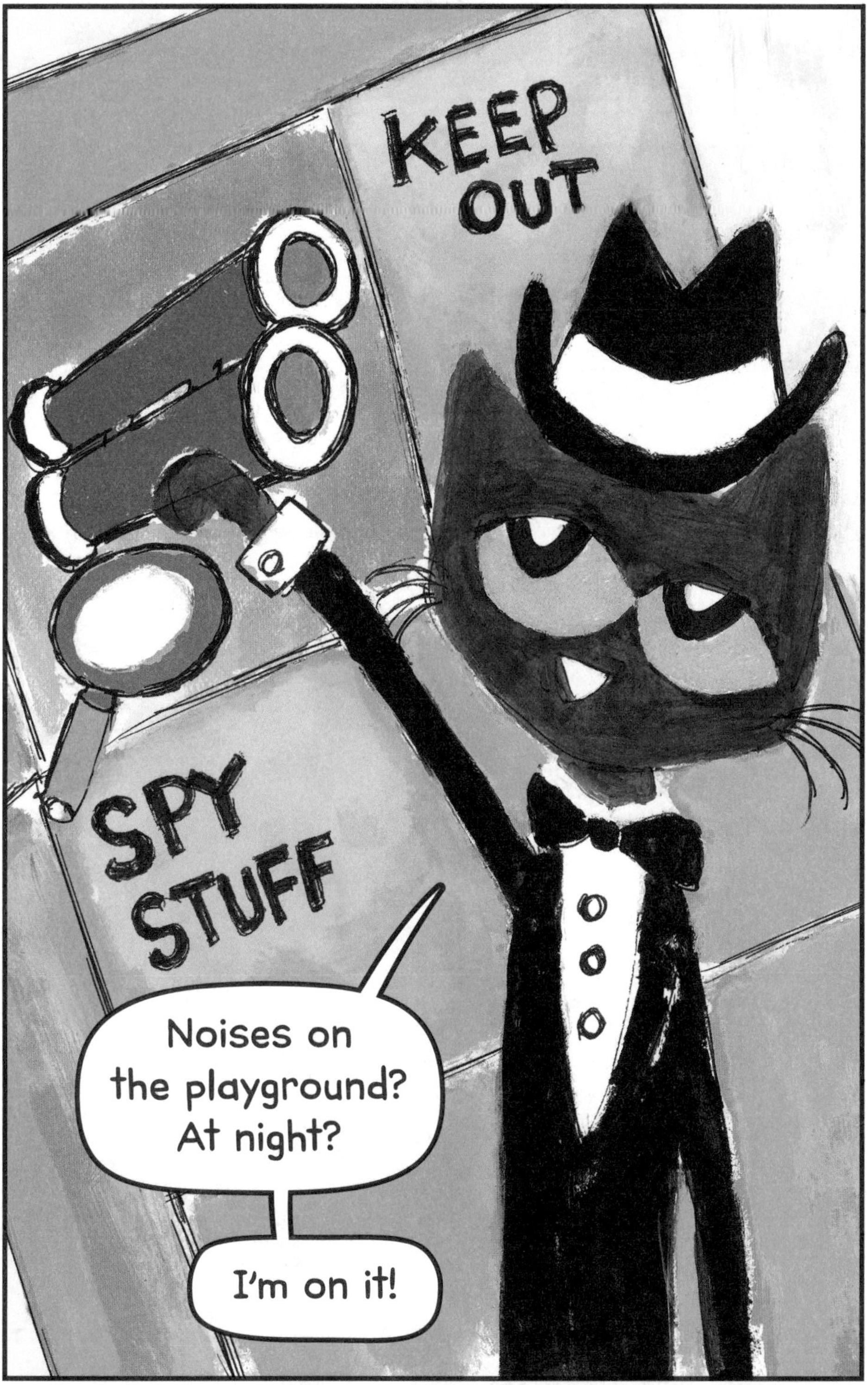
KEEP OUT
SPY STUFF
Noises on the playground? At night?
I'm on it!

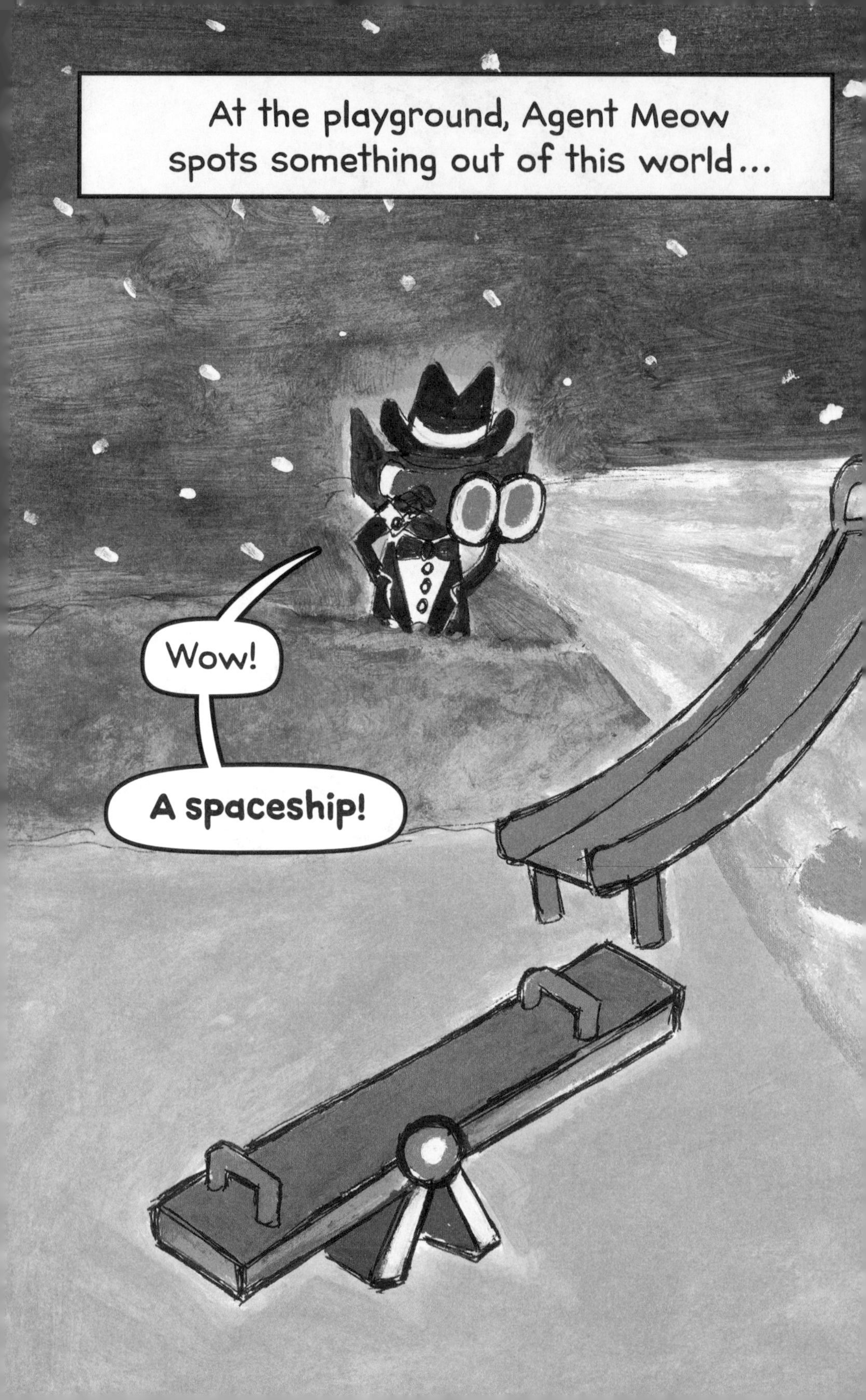
At the playground, Agent Meow spots something out of this world...
Wow!
A spaceship!

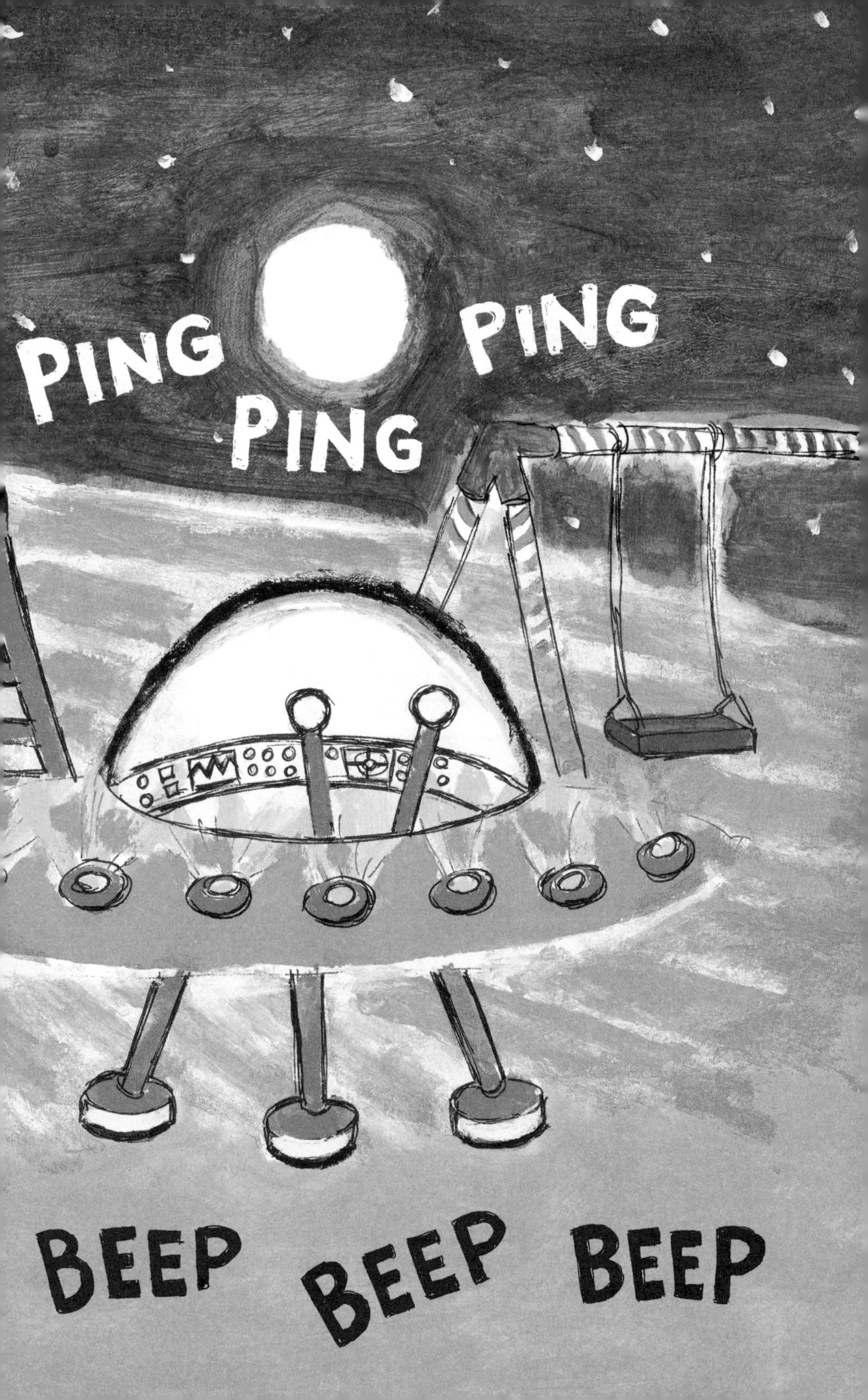
PING
PING
PING
BEEP
BEEP
BEEP

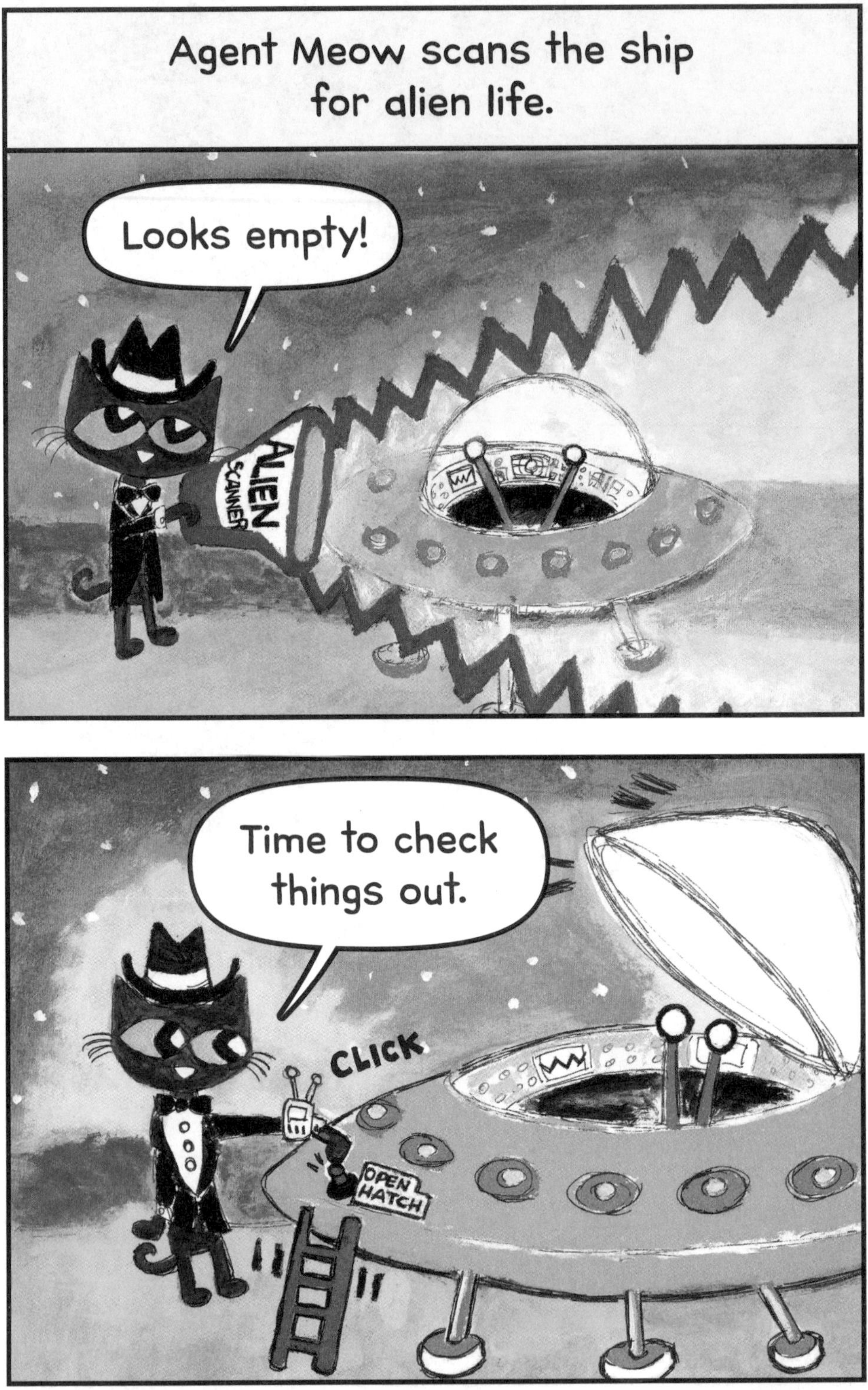
Agent Meow scans the ship for alien life.
Looks empty!
ALIEN SCANNER
Time to check things out.
CLICK
OPEN HATCH

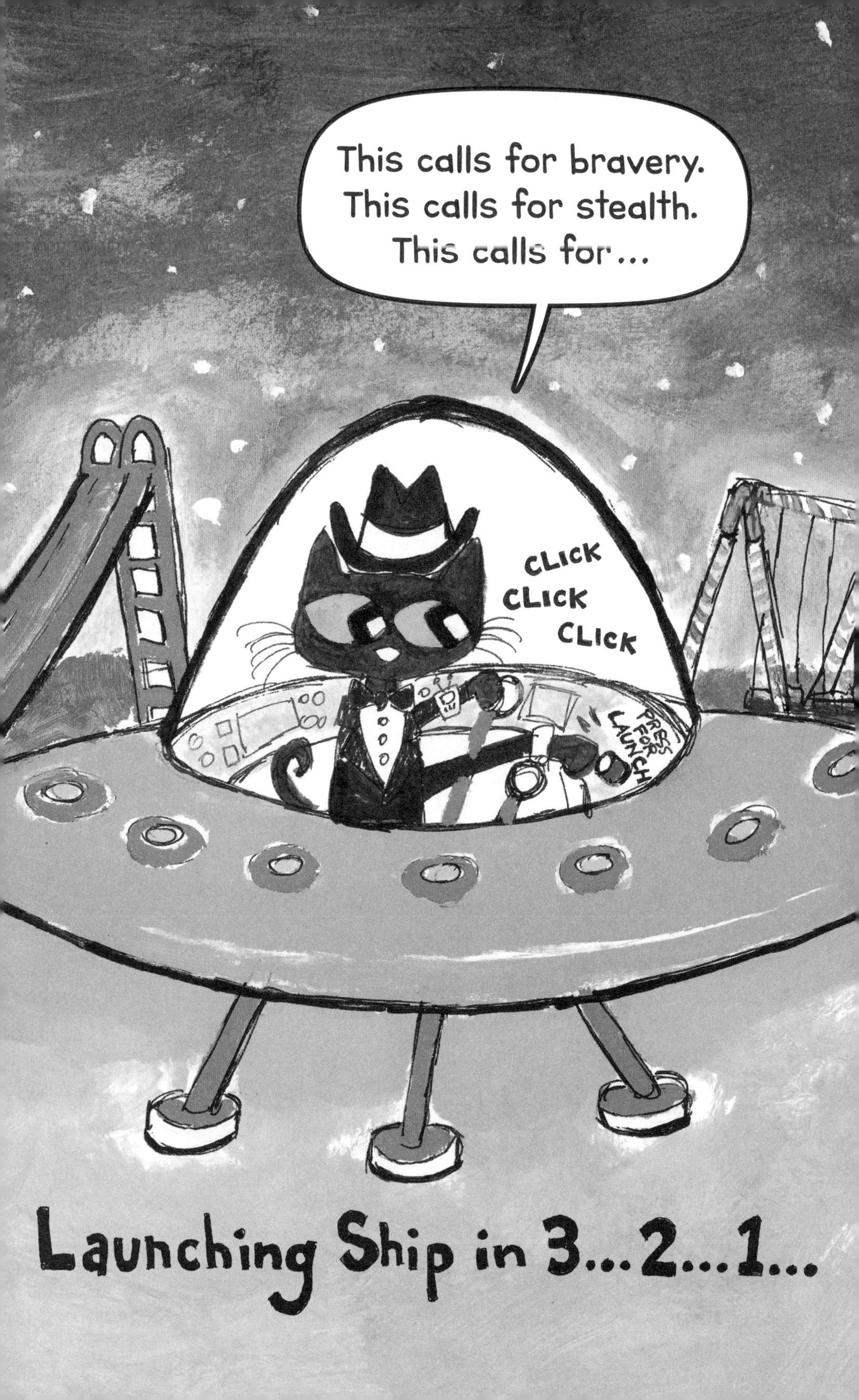
This calls for bravery. This calls for stealth. This calls for...
CLICK
CLICK
CLICK
PRESS FOR LAUNCH
Launching Ship in 3...2...1...

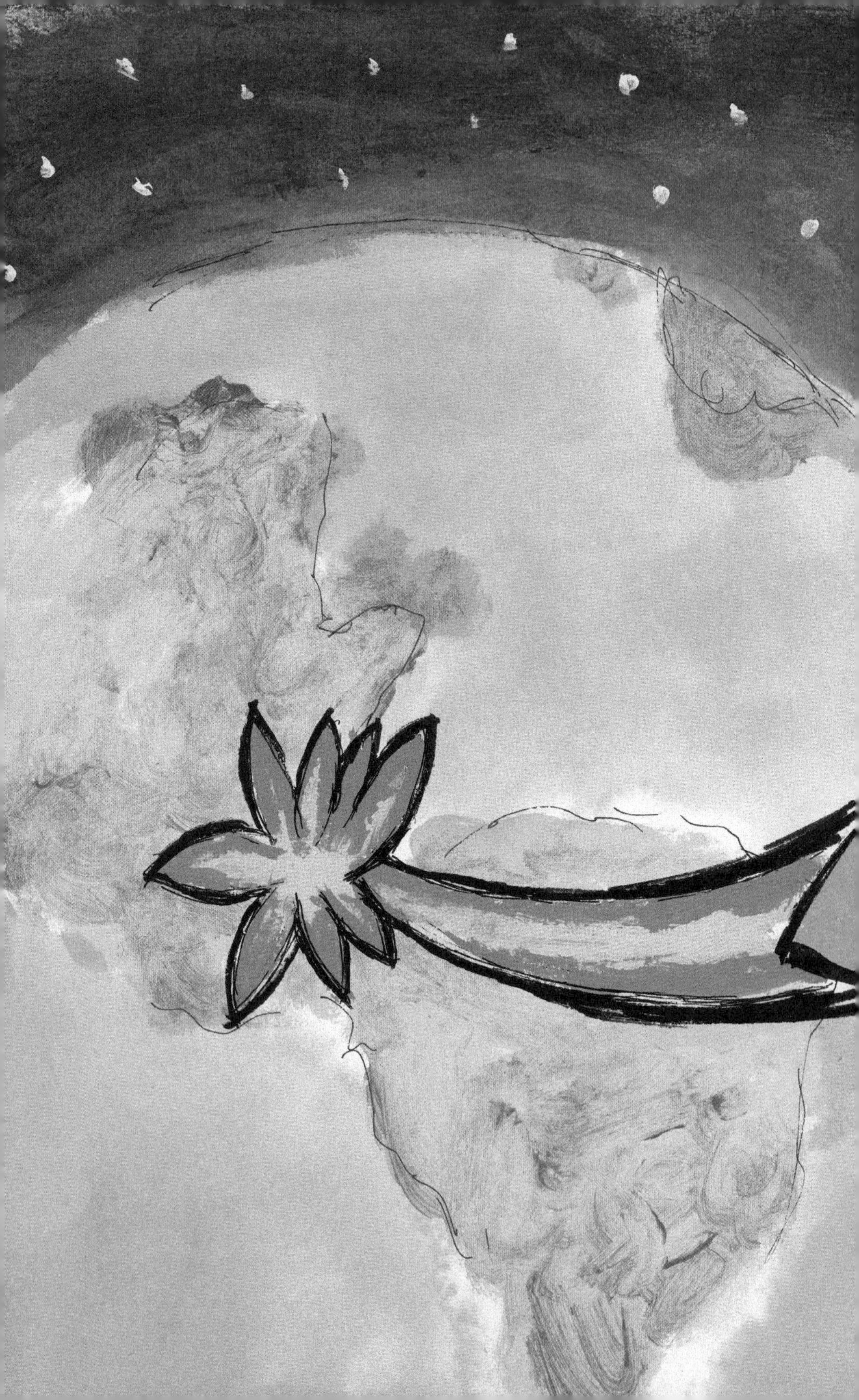

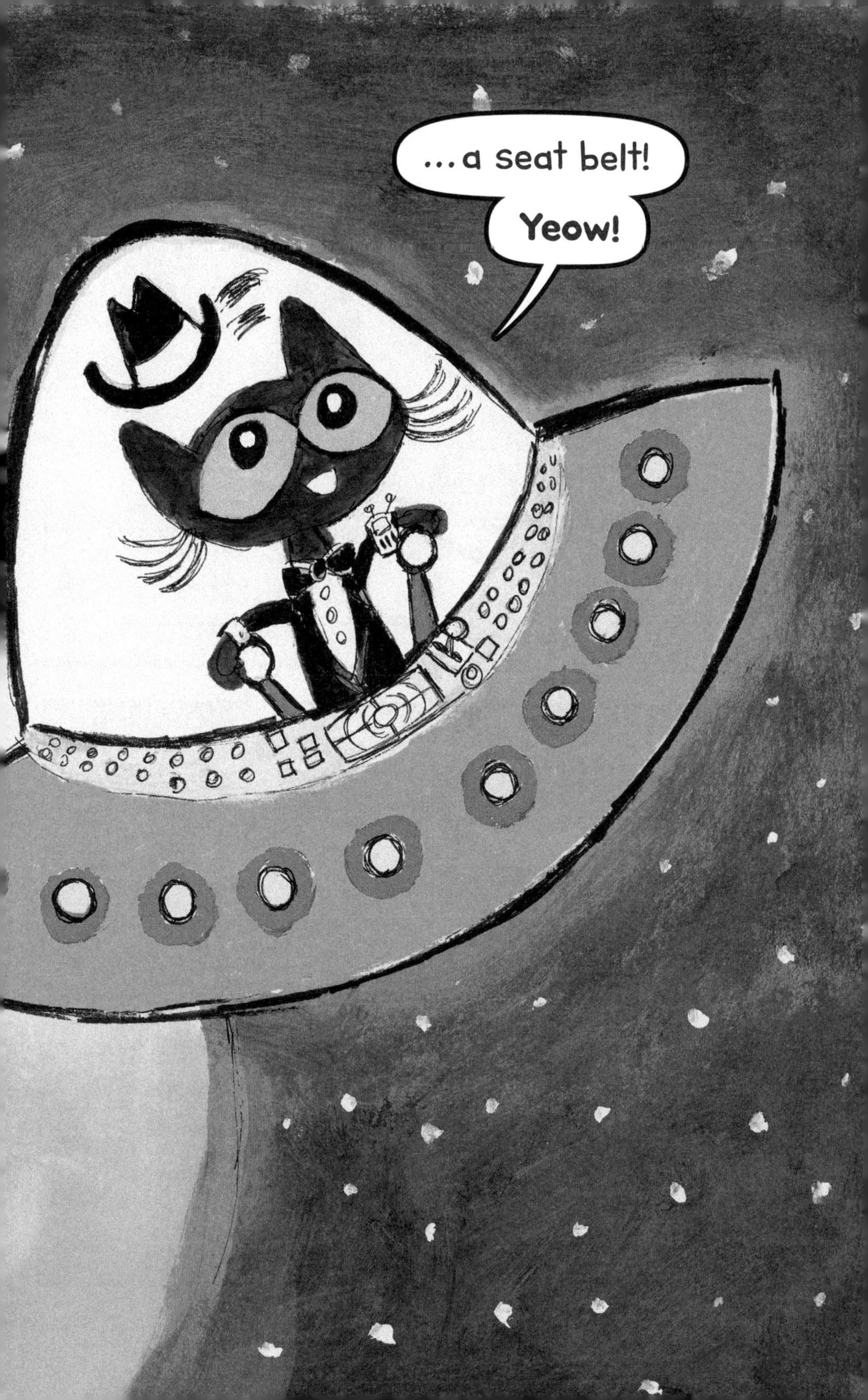
...a seat belt!
Yeow!

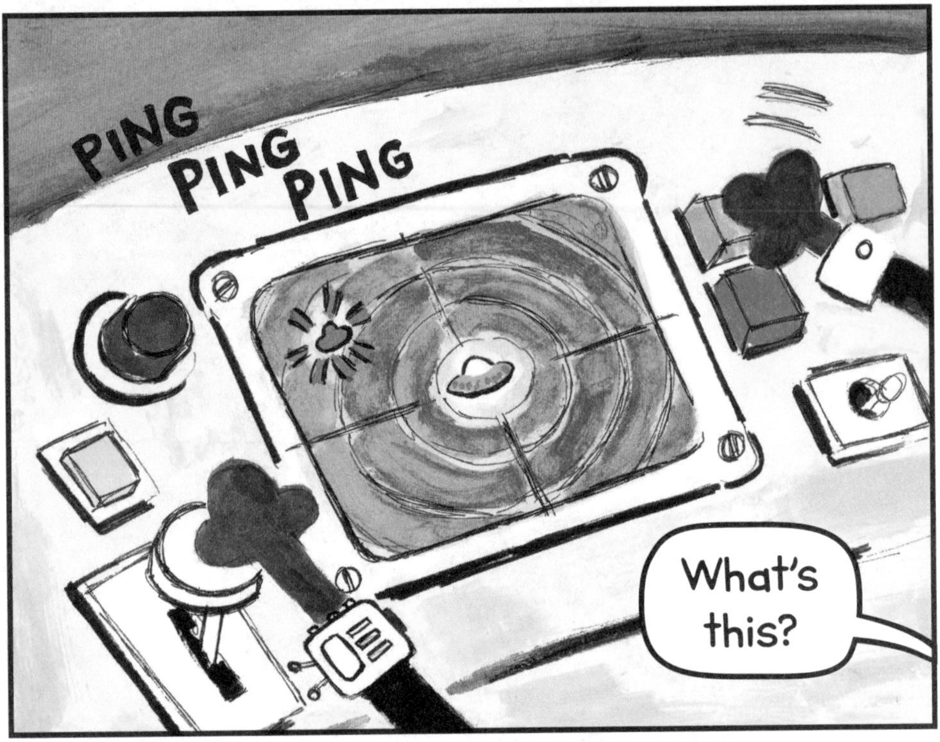
PING
PING
PING
What's this?

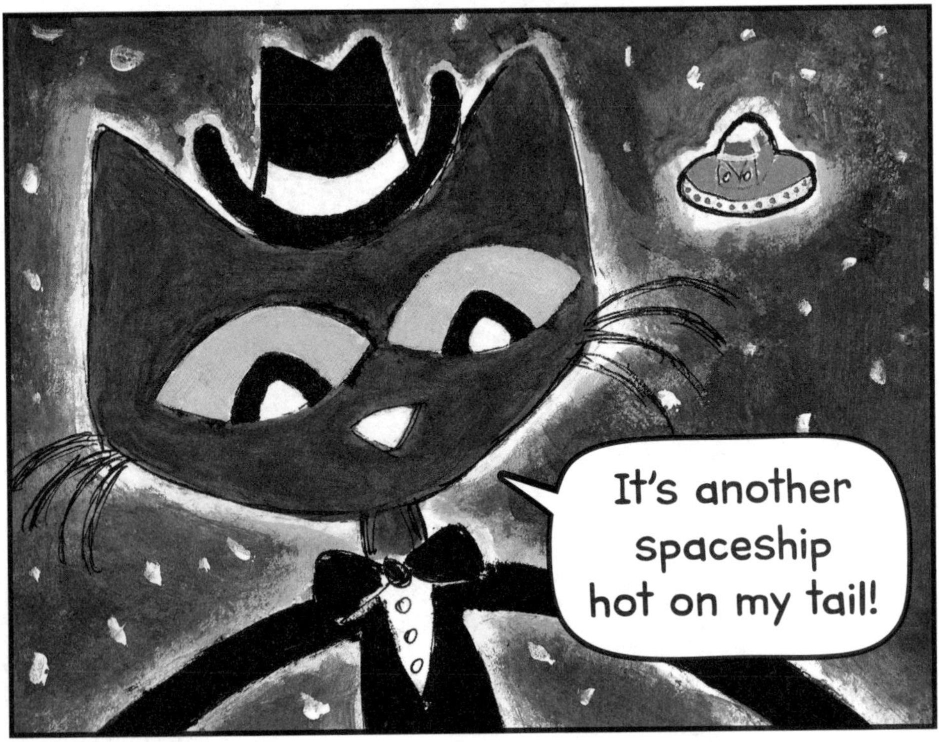
It's another spaceship hot on my tail!

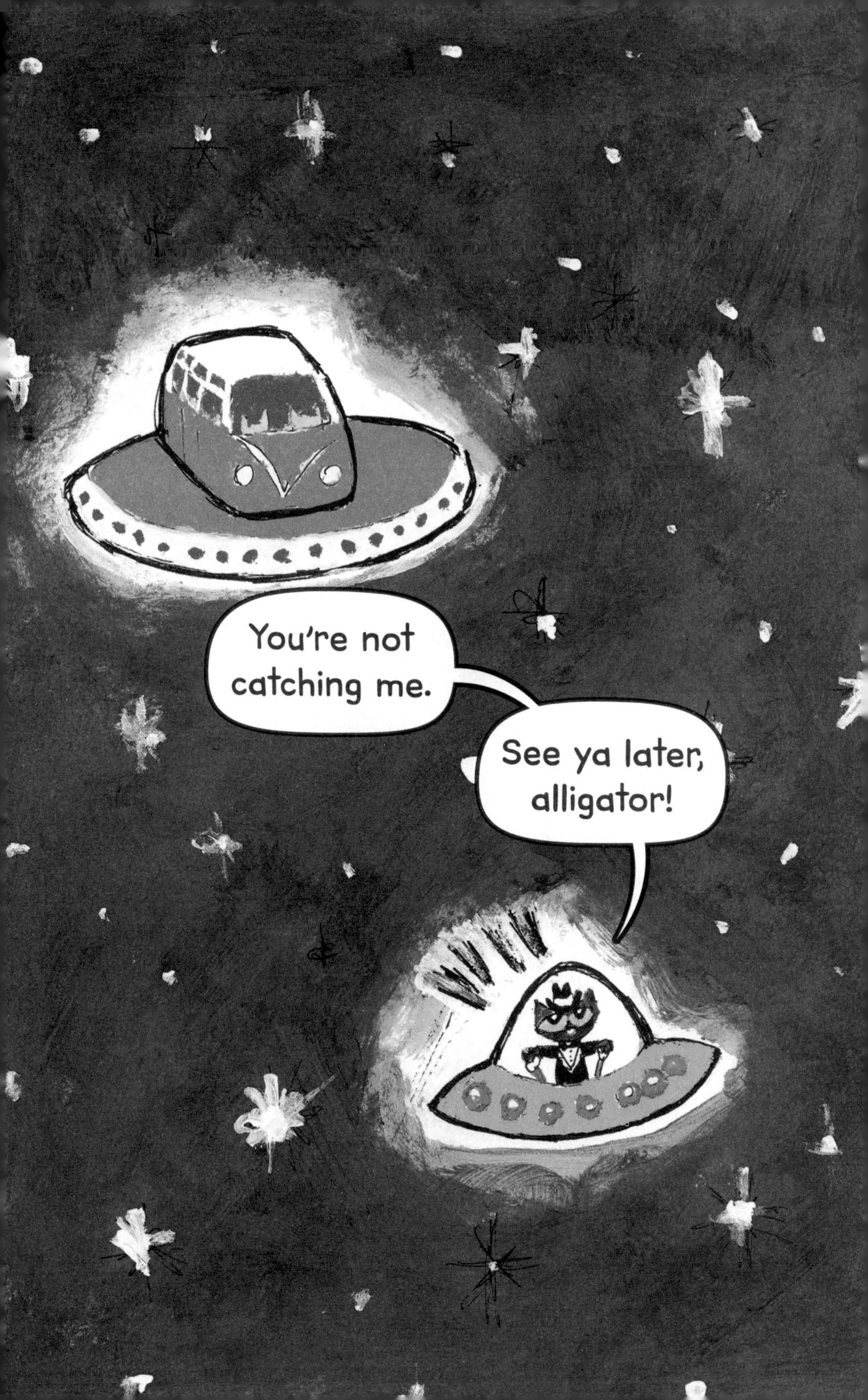
You're not catching me.
See ya later, alligator!

Agent Meow zips past Mars.

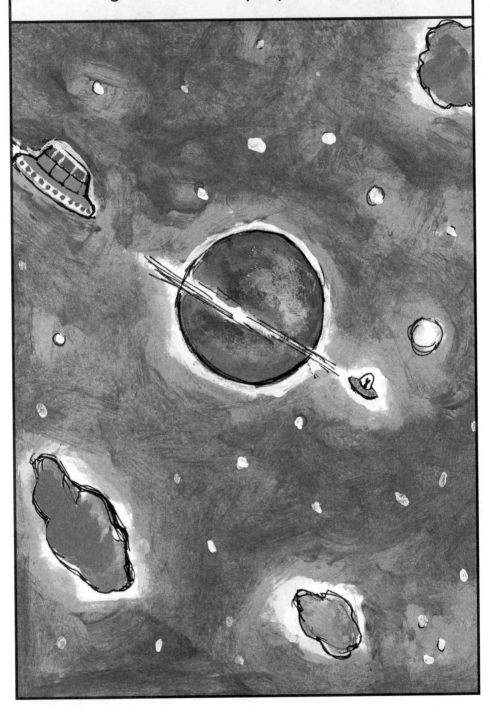

He zooms past Jupiter.

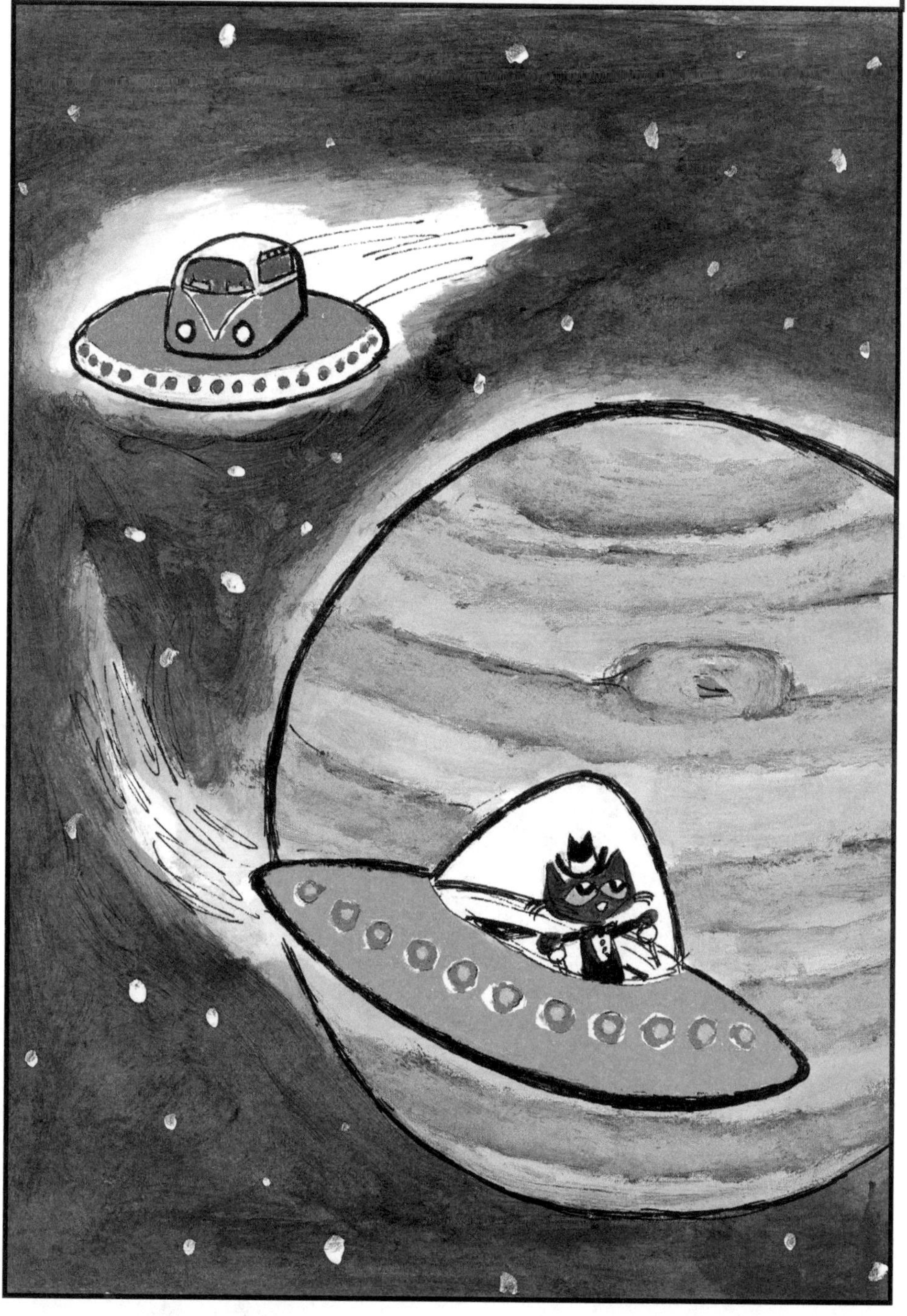

Agent Meow dodges flying rocks
and soars past Saturn.
But he cannot get away
from the spaceship.

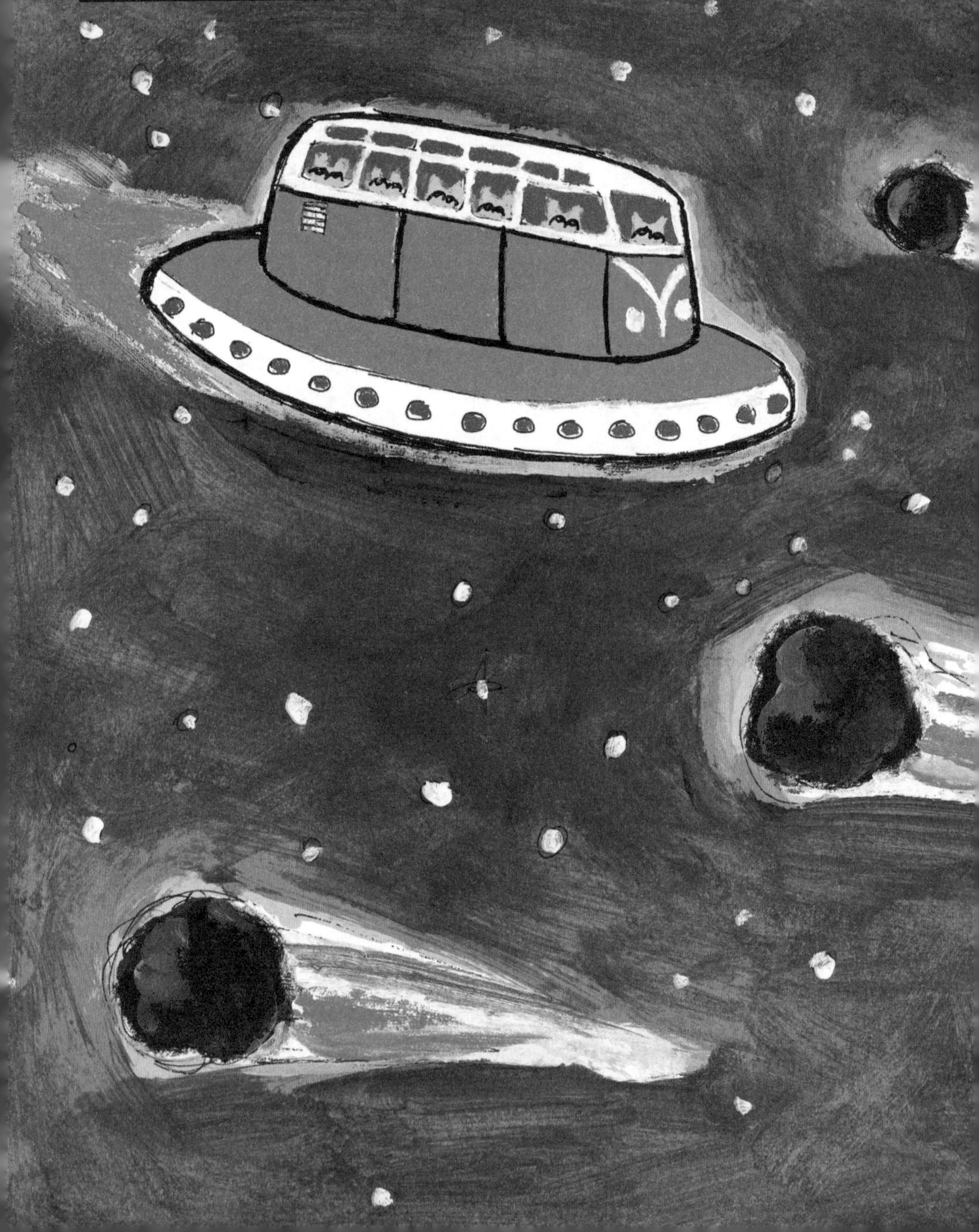

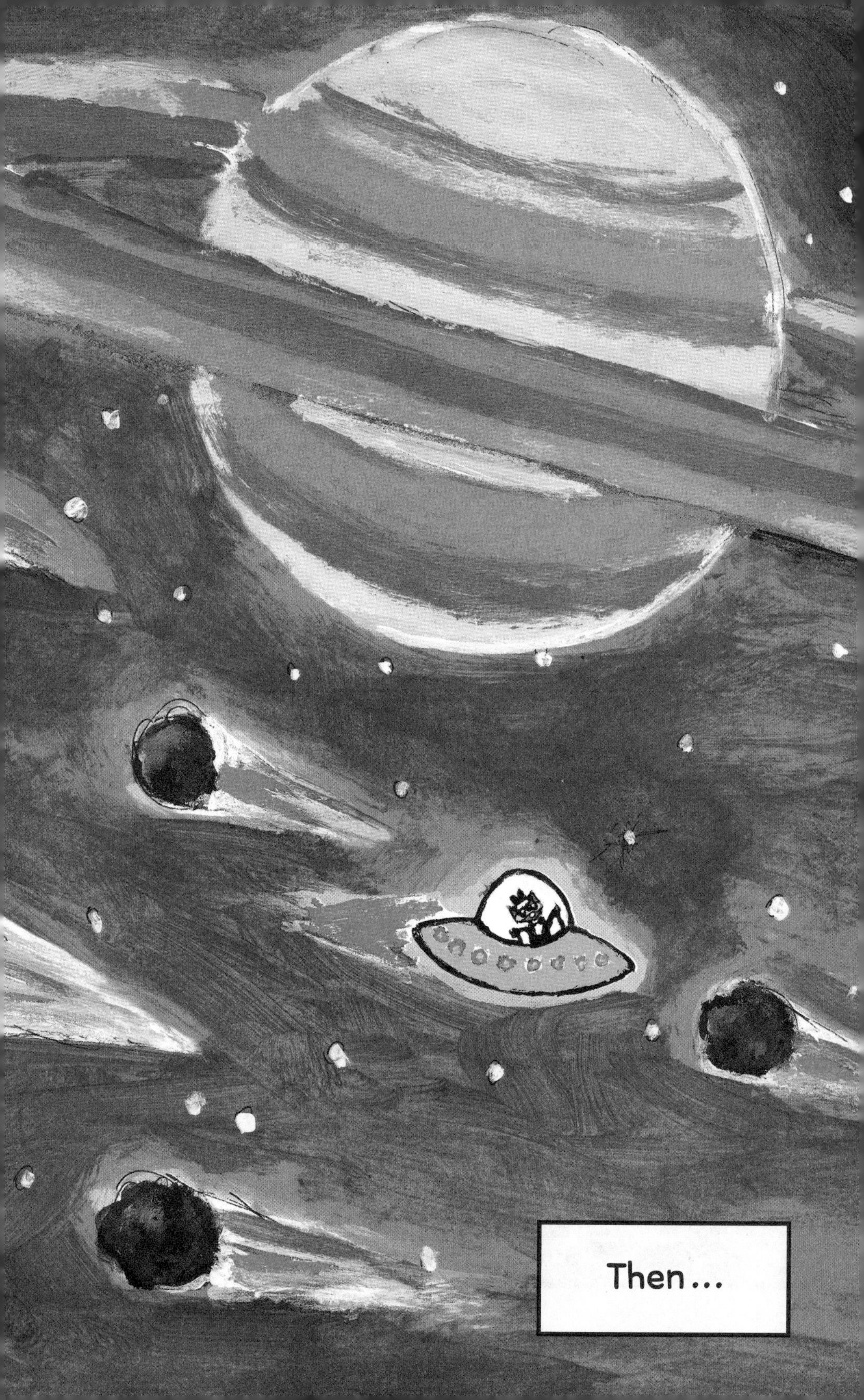
Then ...

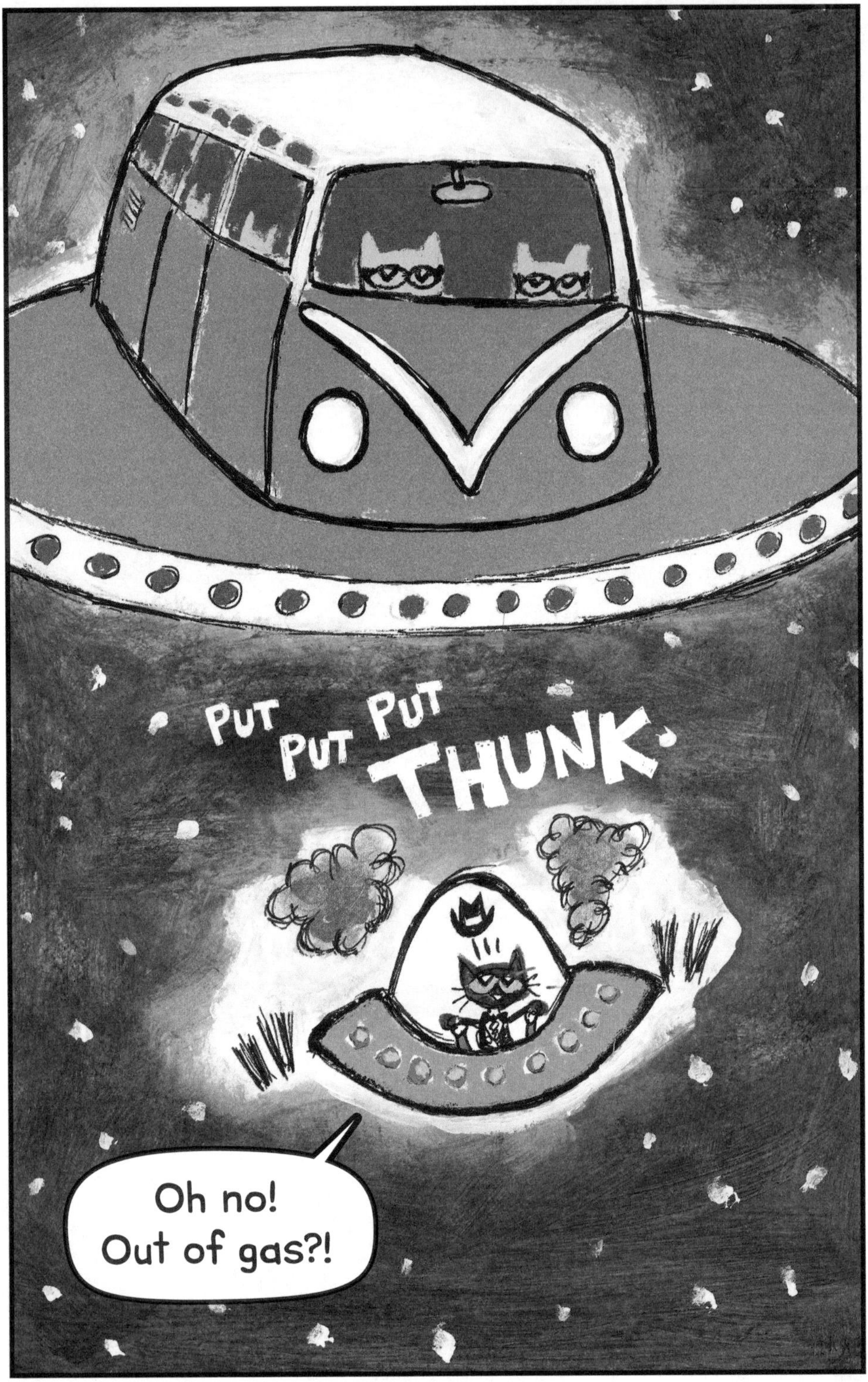
PUT PUT PUT THUNK
Oh no!
Out of gas?!

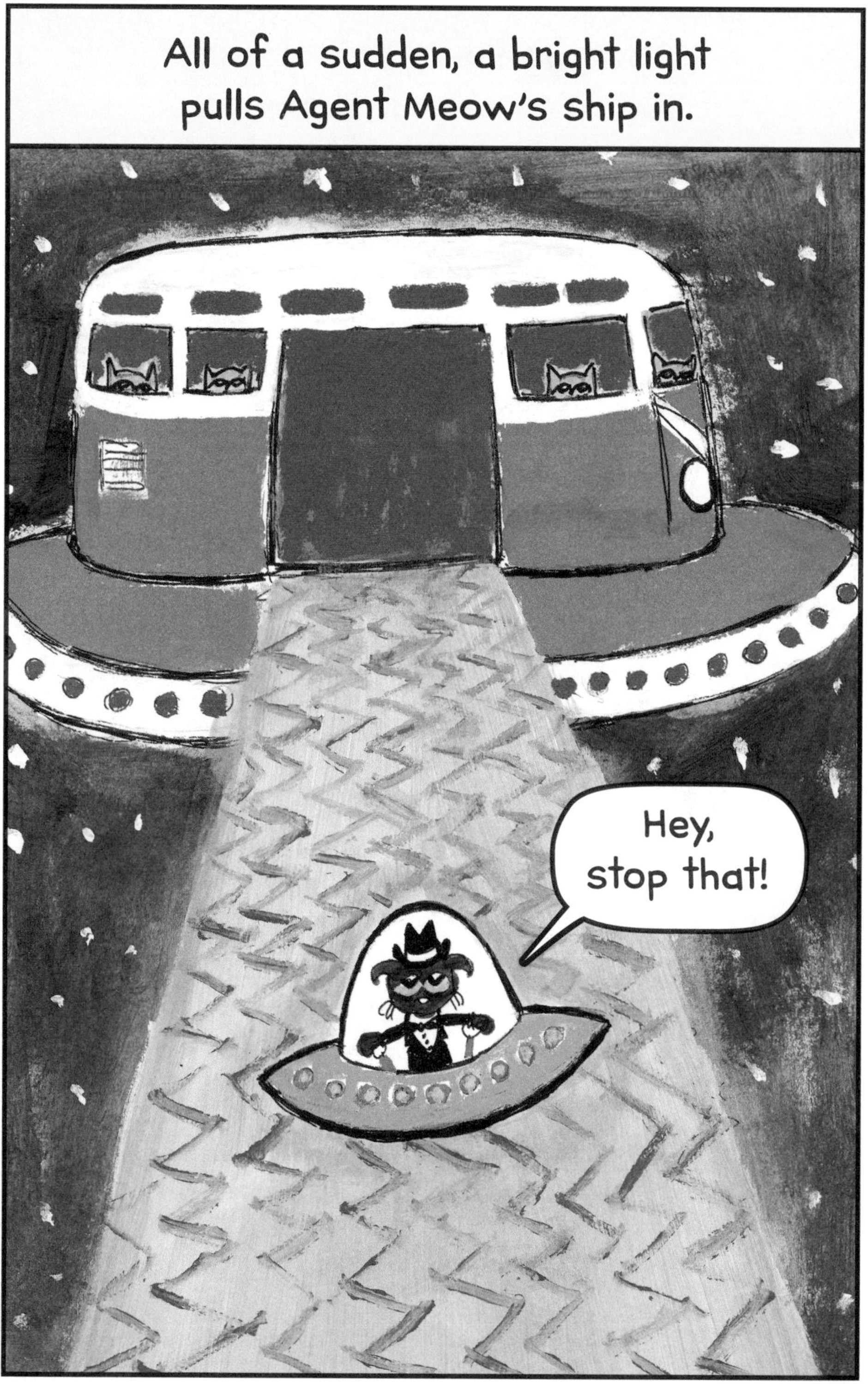
All of a sudden, a bright light pulls Agent Meow's ship in.
Hey, stop that!

Agent Meow's ship docks.
The door begins to open...

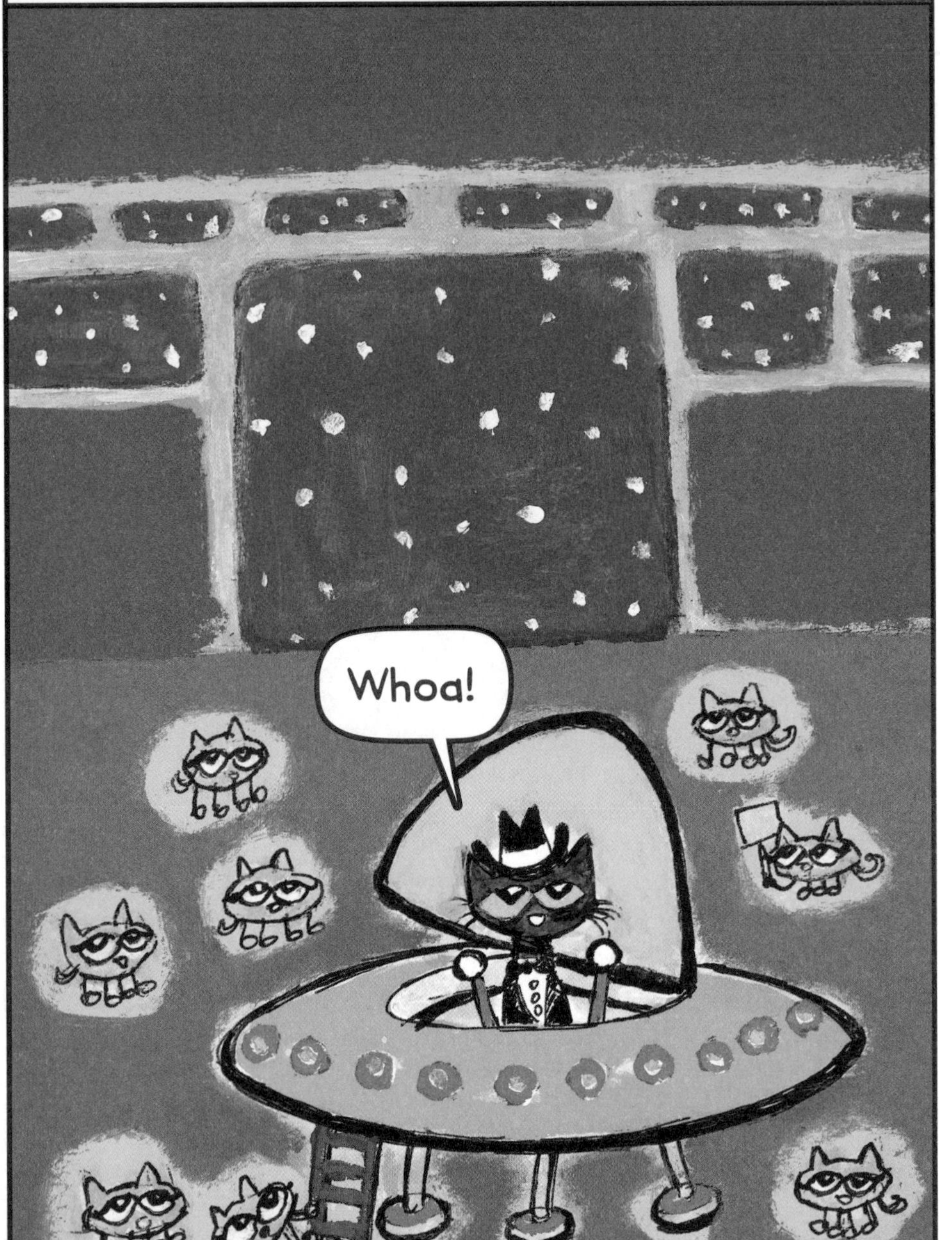
Whoa!

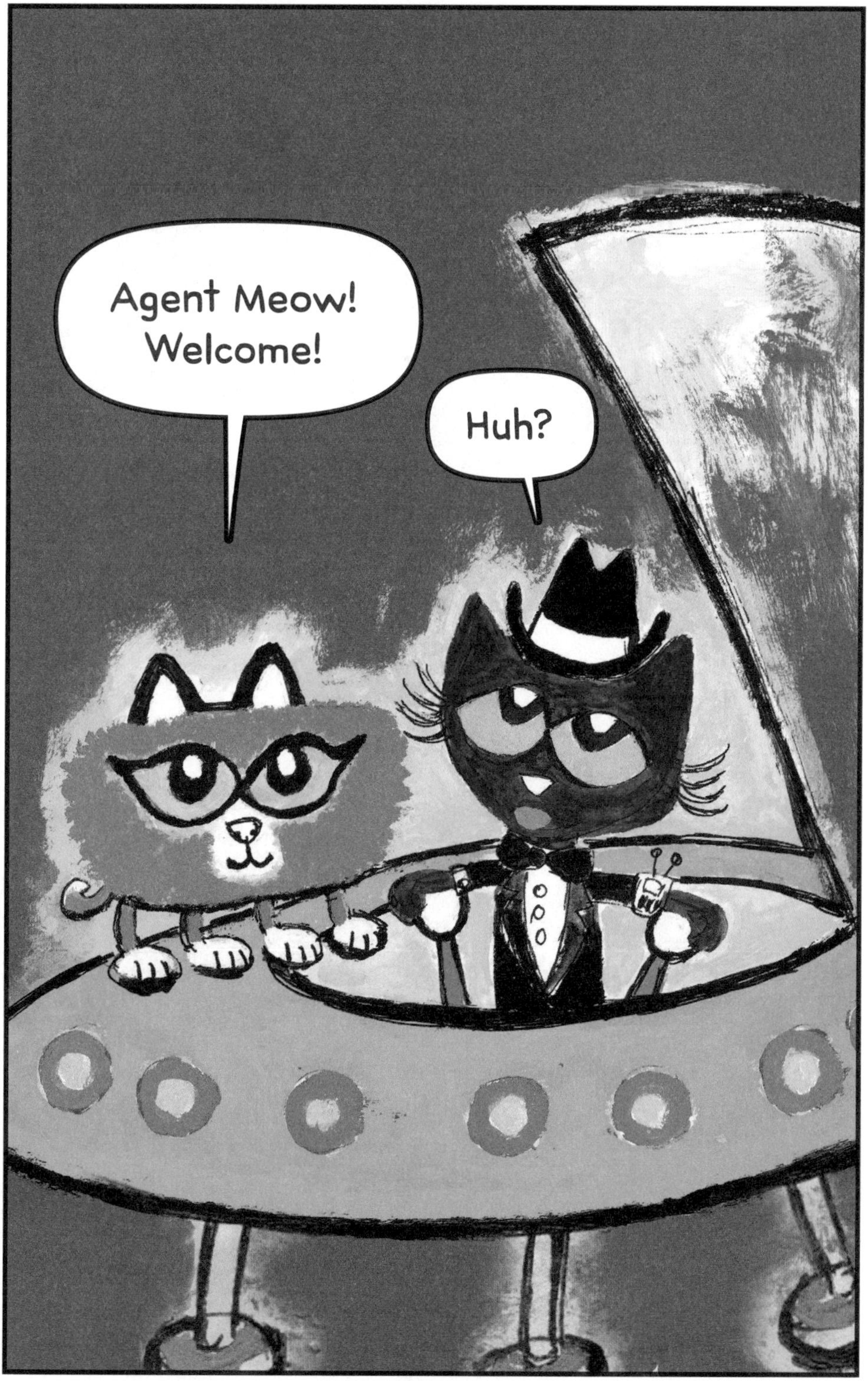
Agent Meow! Welcome!
Huh?

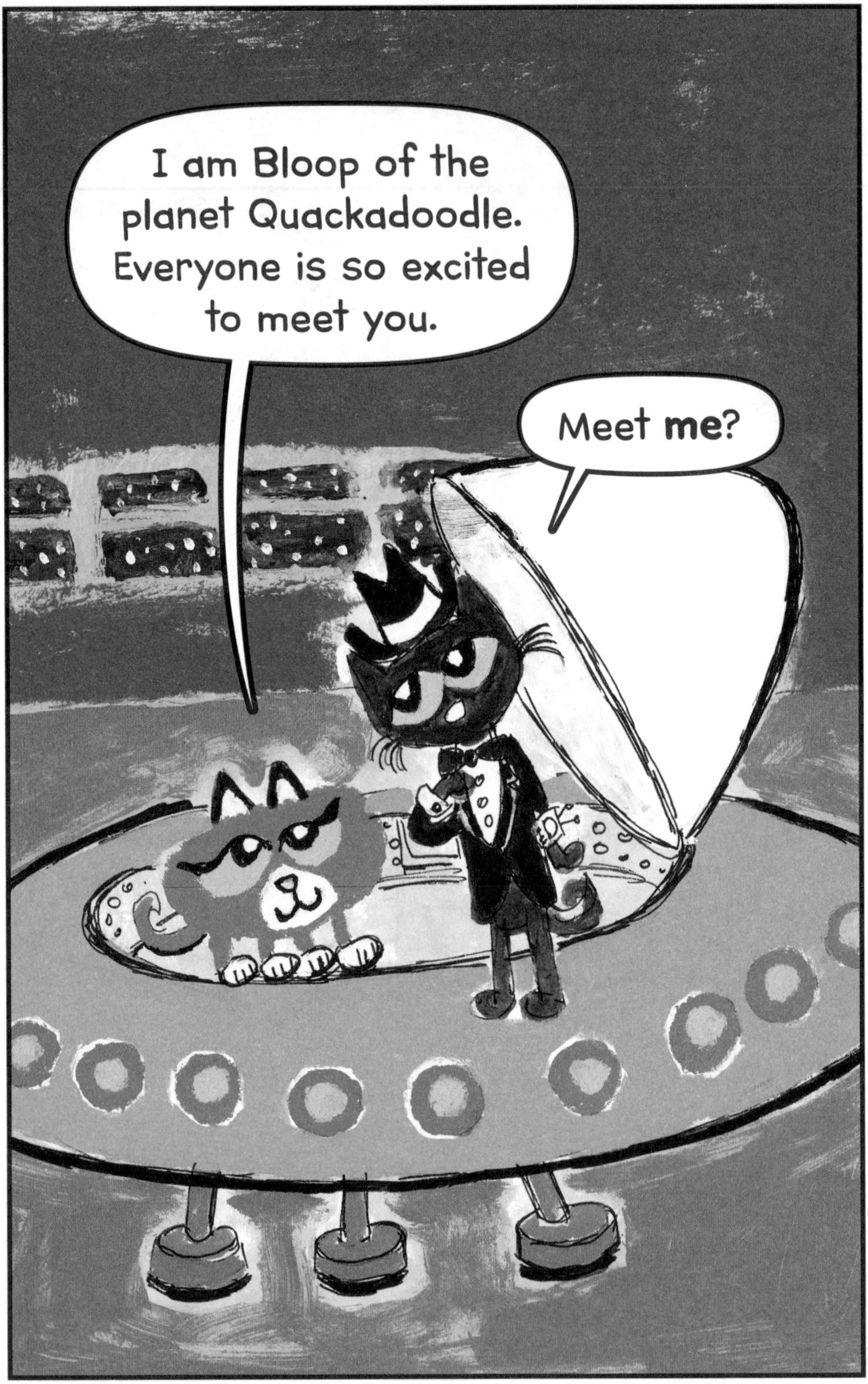
I am Bloop of the planet Quackadoodle. Everyone is so excited to meet you.
Meet **me**?

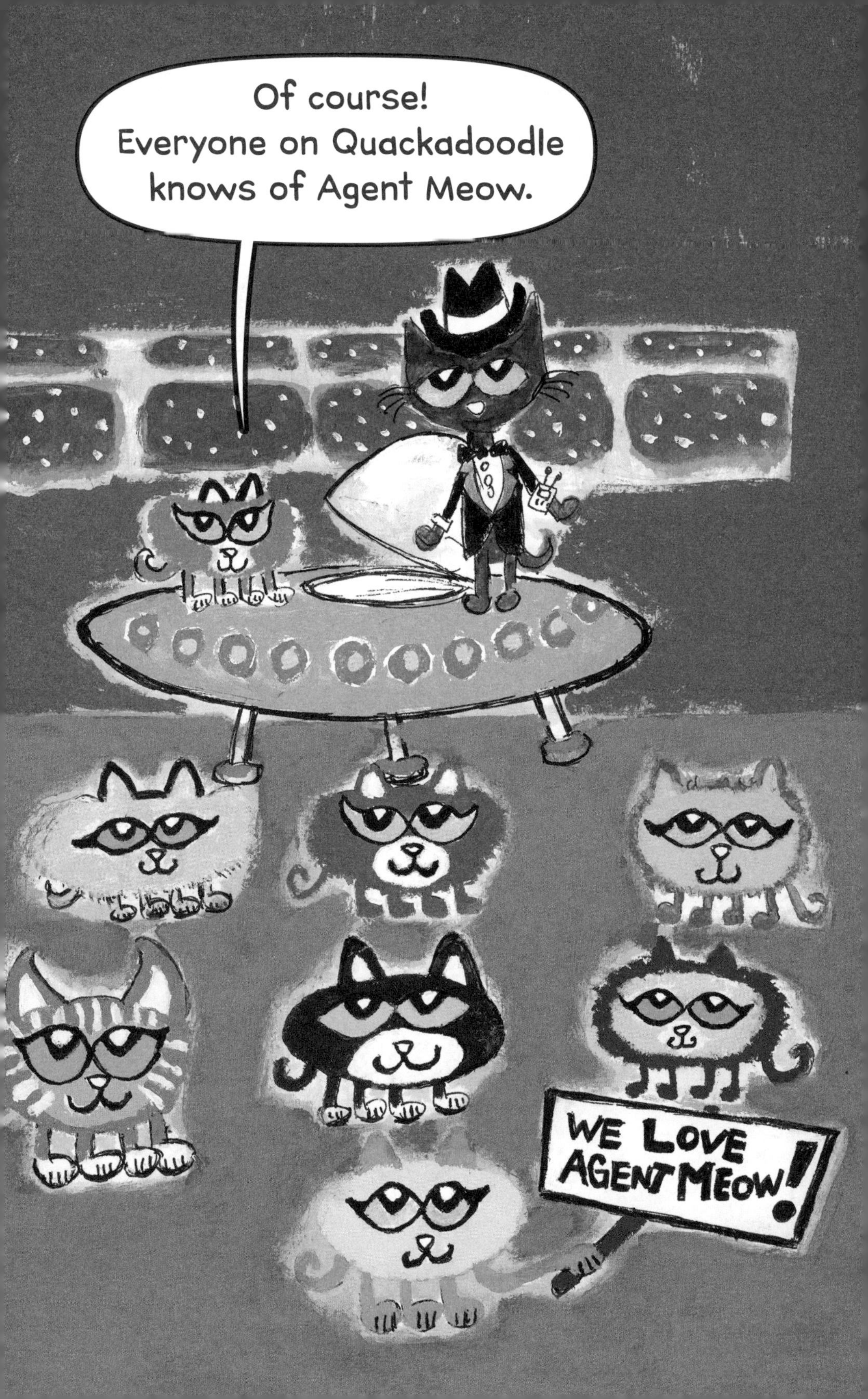
Of course! Everyone on Quackadoodle knows of Agent Meow.
WE LOVE AGENT MEOW!

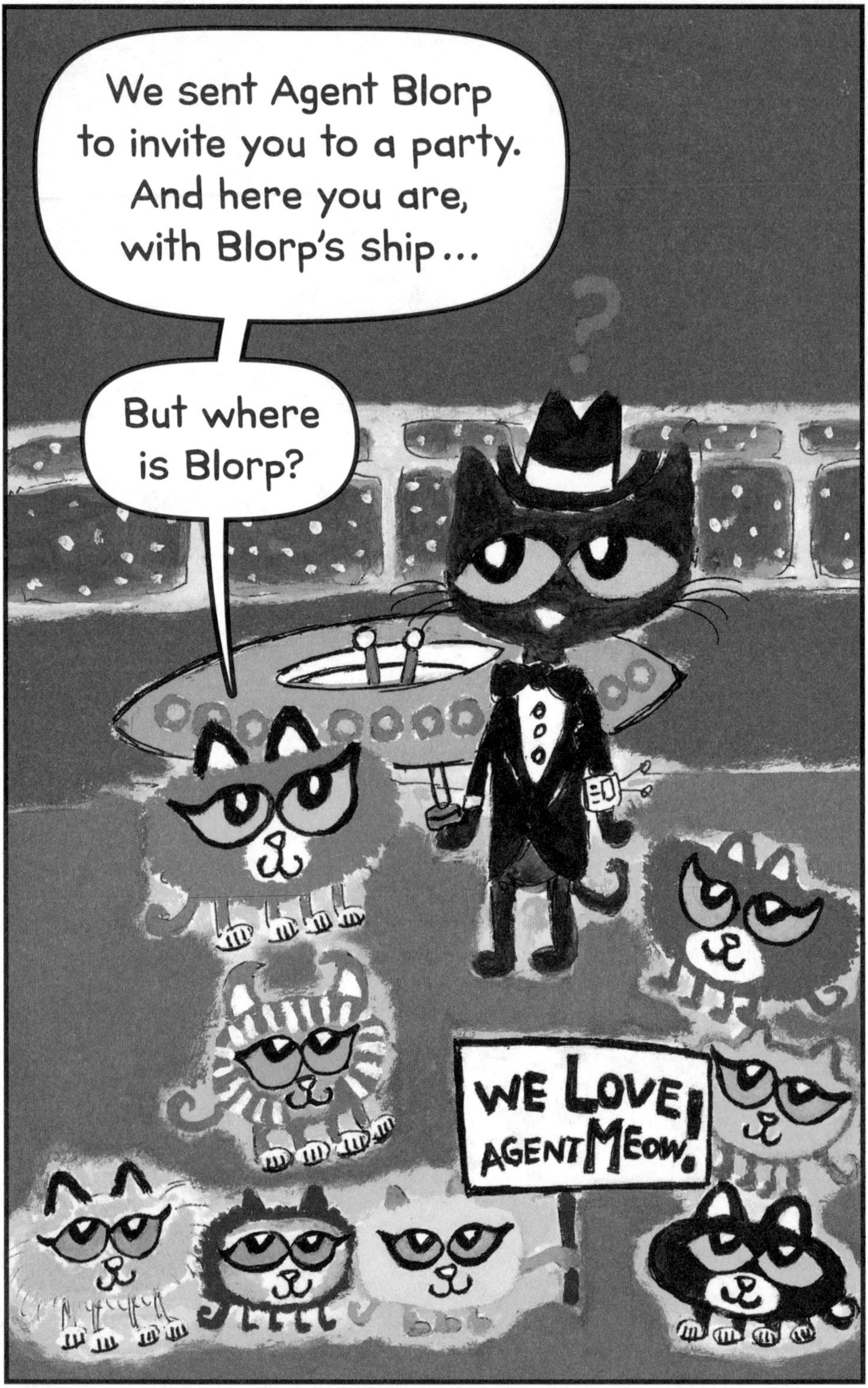
We sent Agent Blorp to invite you to a party. And here you are, with Blorp's ship...
But where is Blorp?
?
WE LOVE AGENT MEOW!

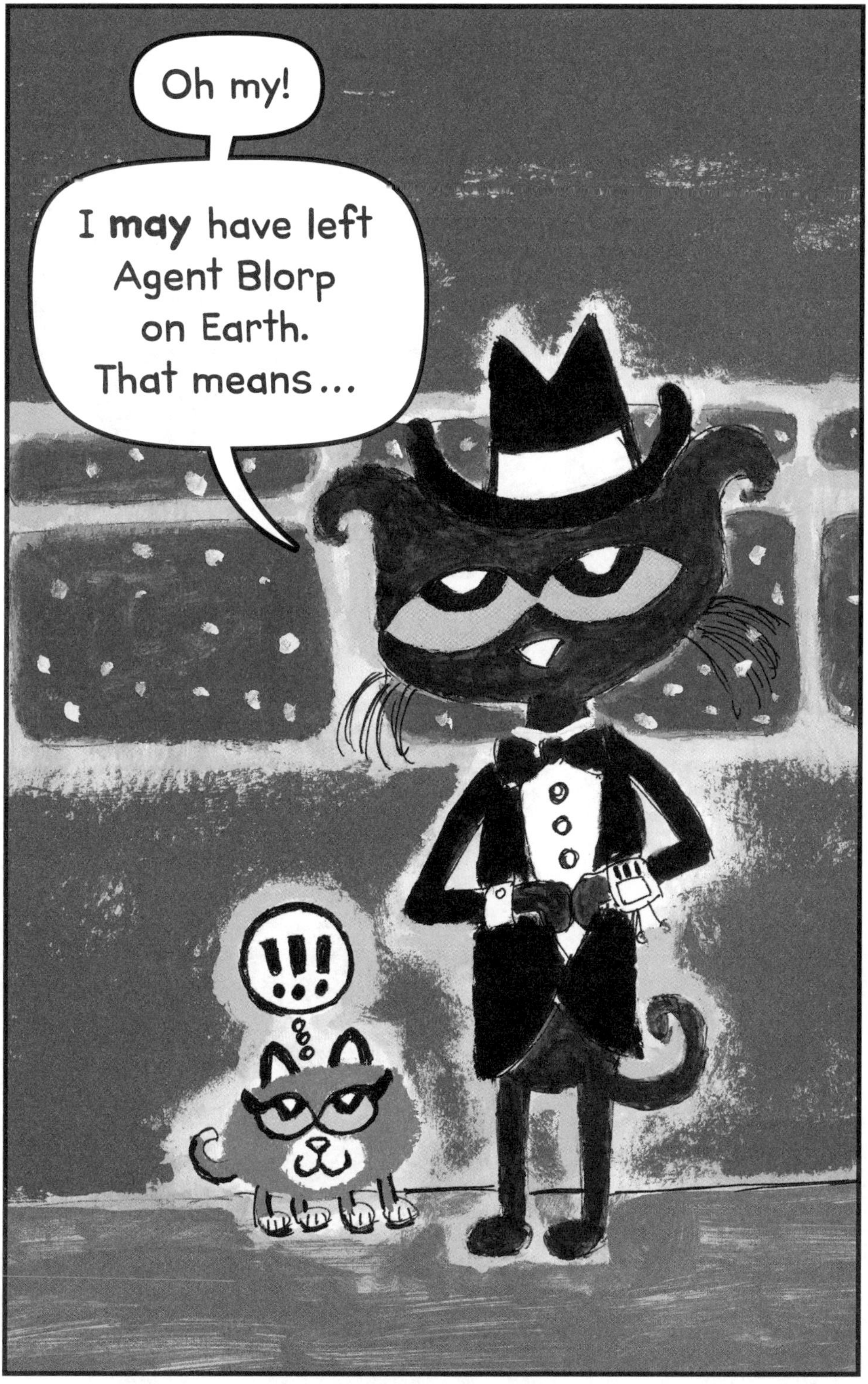
Oh my!
I **may** have left Agent Blorp on Earth. That means...
!!!

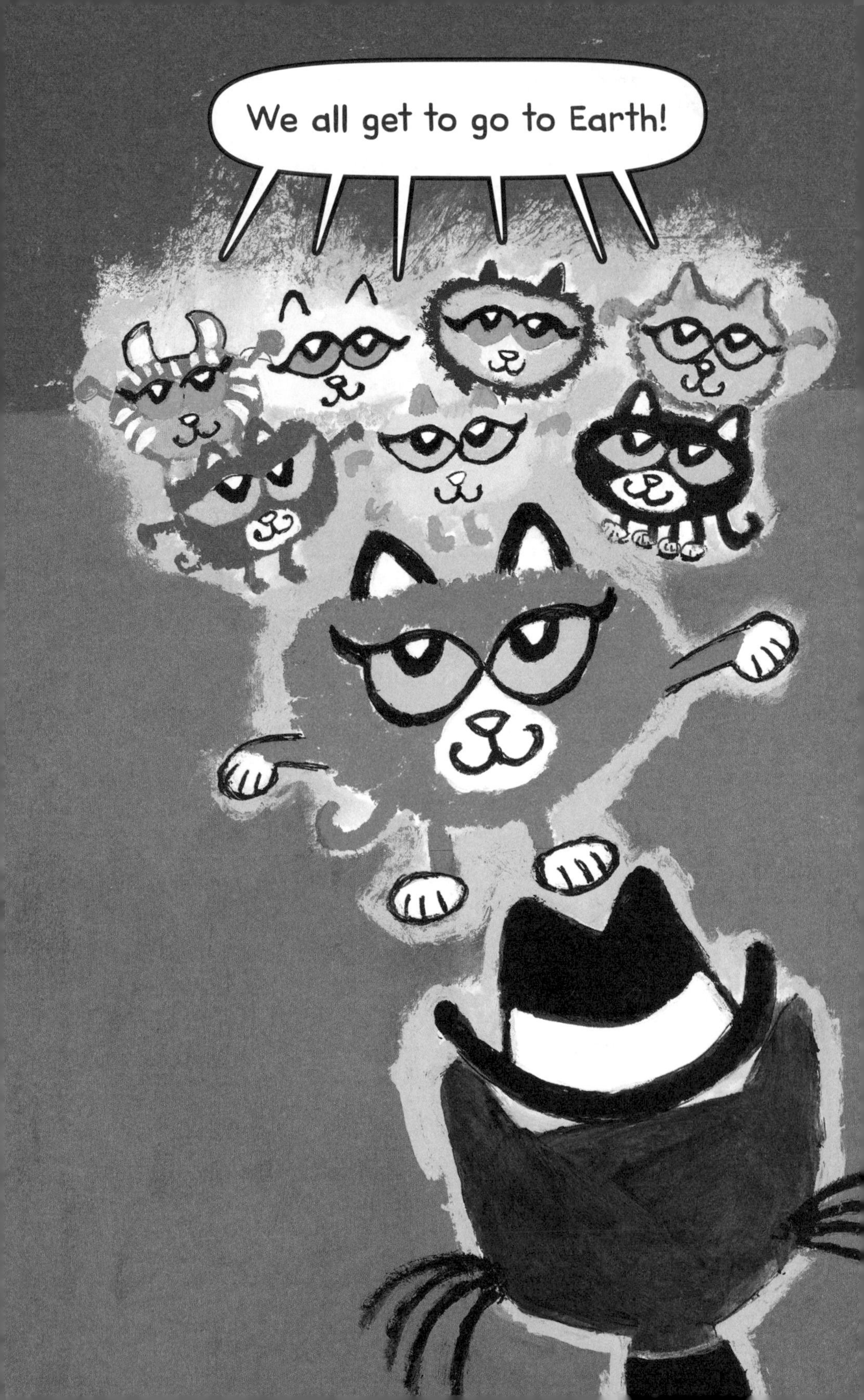
We all get to go to Earth!

One spaceship ride later ...

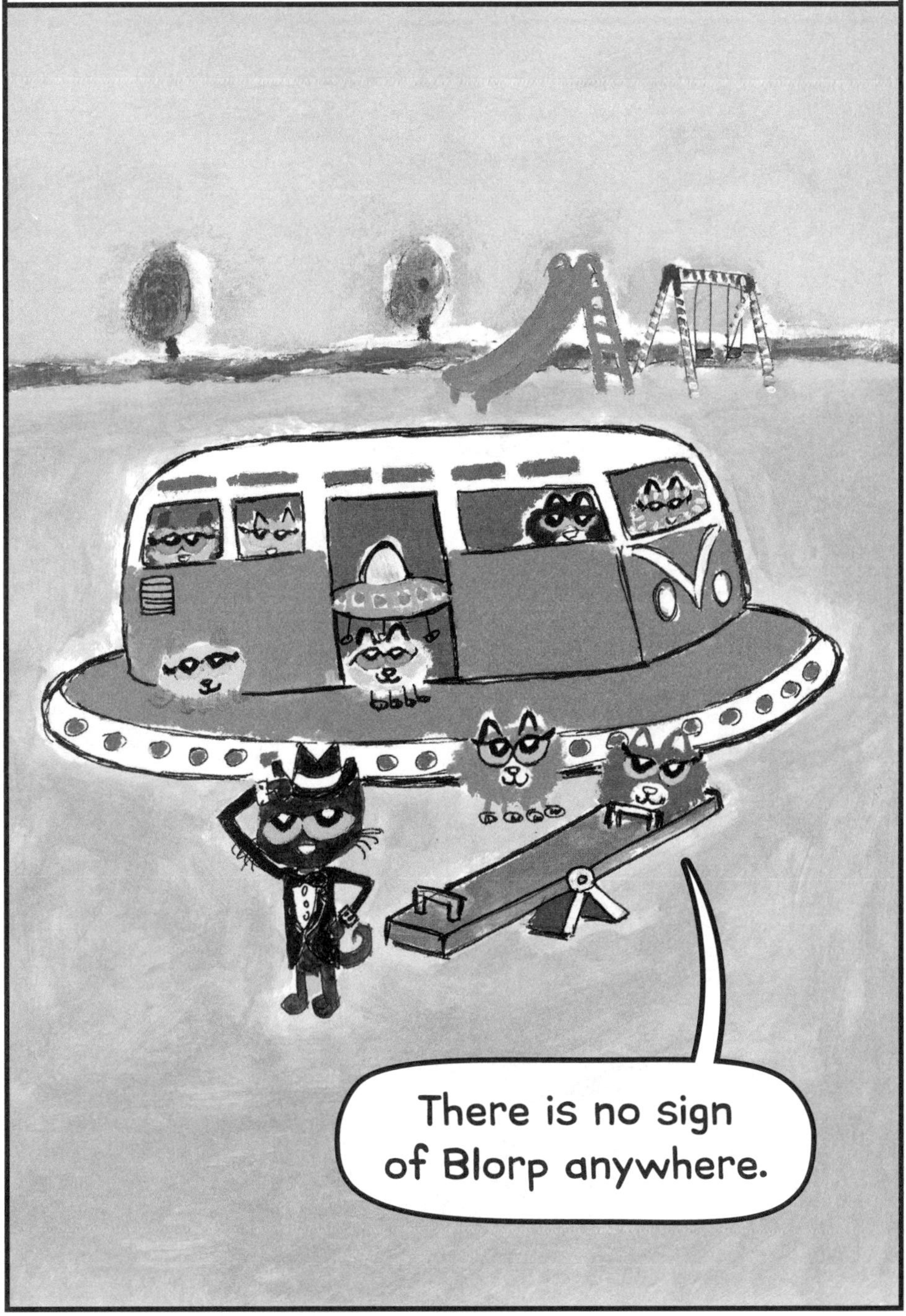
There is no sign of Blorp anywhere.

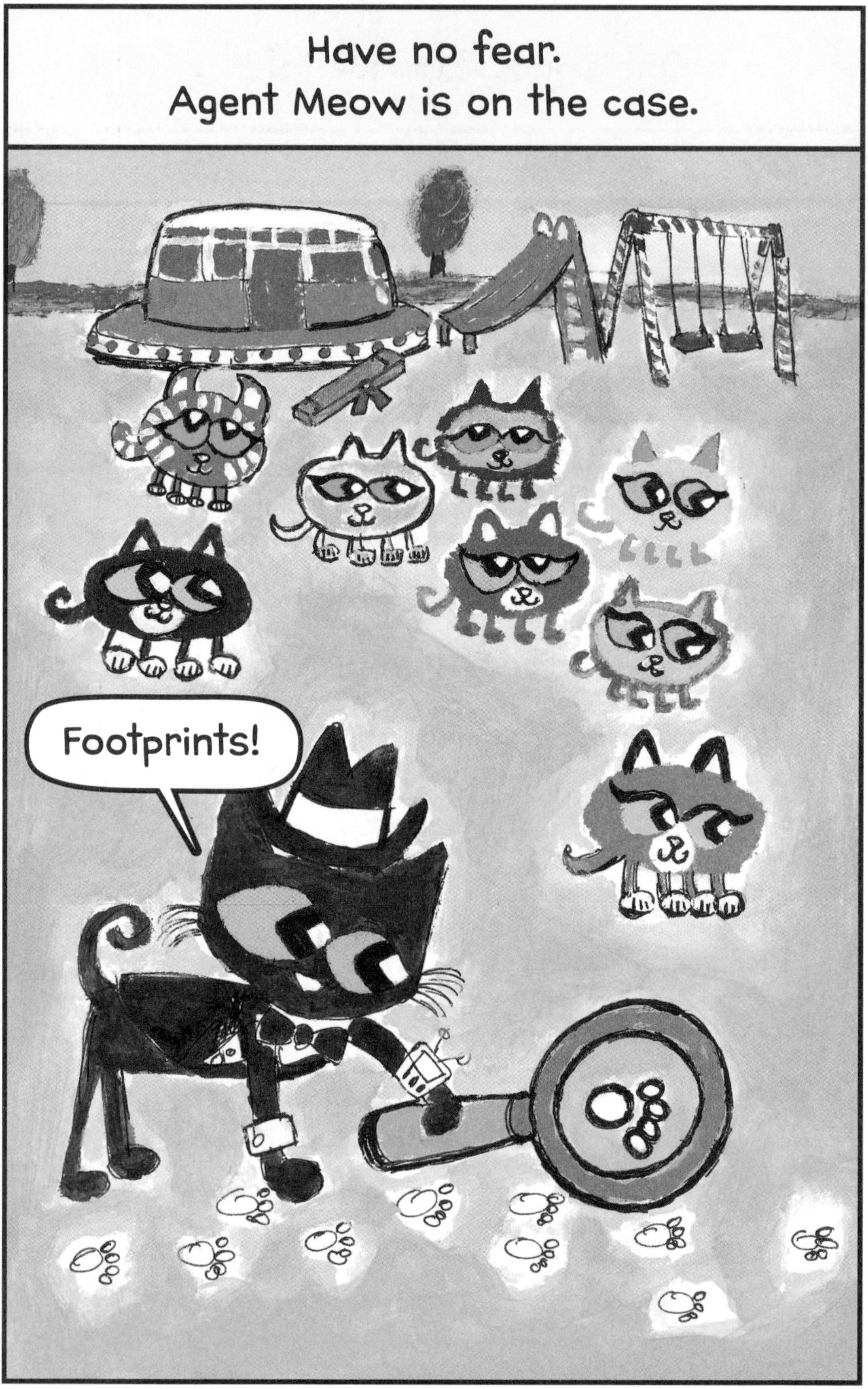
Have no fear.
Agent Meow is on the case.
Footprints!

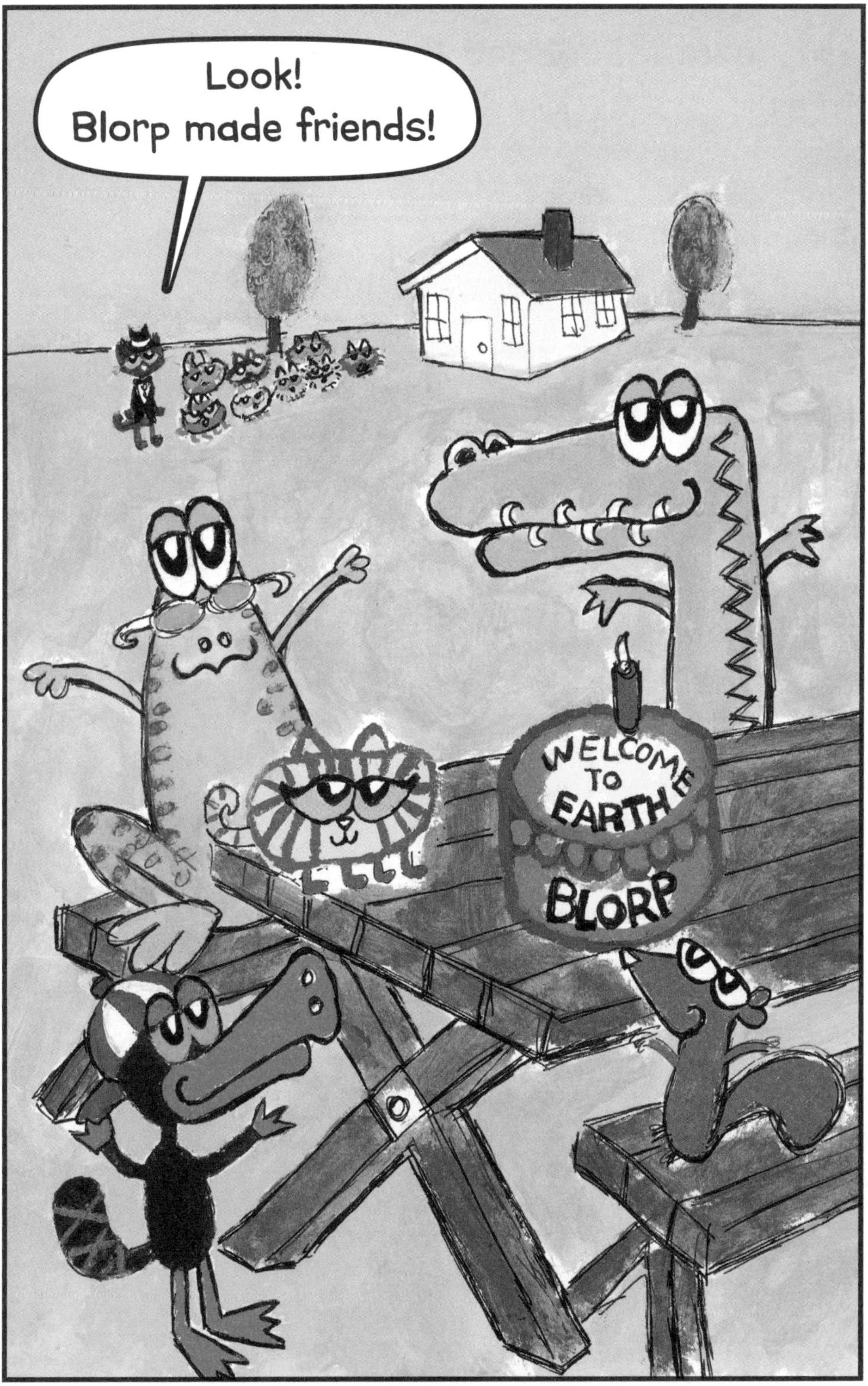
Look!
Blorp made friends!
WELCOME TO EARTH
BLORP

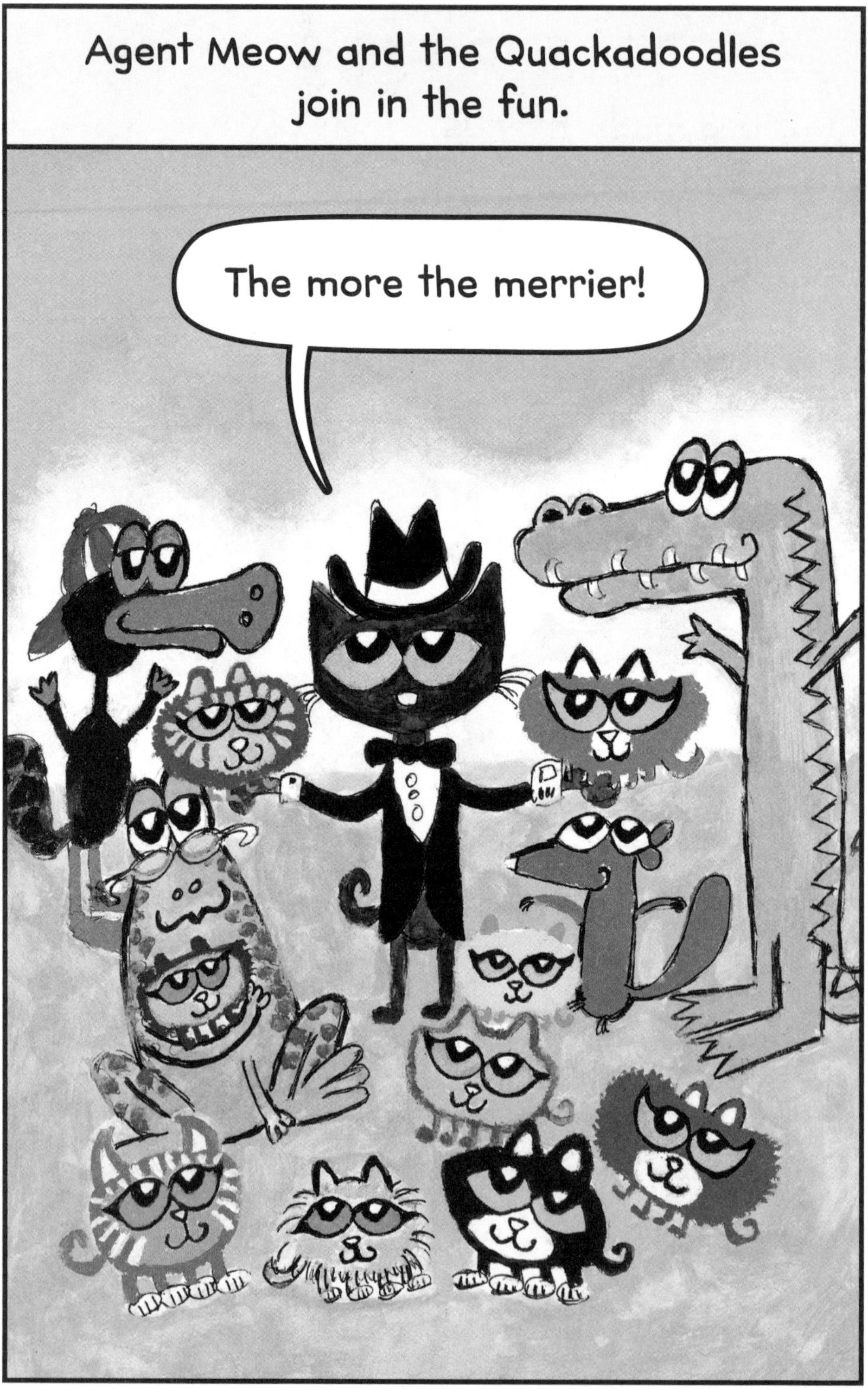
Agent Meow and the Quackadoodles join in the fun.
The more the merrier!